THIS BOOK BELONGS
TO :
Sarah Morgan Stadler

THE TALE OF
THE FAITHFUL DOVE

*This little story was written by Beatrix Potter
at Hastings, Sussex, England, in 1907.
She wrote of the story:
"This story is true but it happened
in another seaside town, I think Folkestone.
I used Winchelsea and Rye
as background."*

THE TALE OF
THE FAITHFUL DOVE

BY BEATRIX POTTER

Author of
"The Tale of Peter Rabbit," etc.

ILLUSTRATED BY
MARIE ANGEL

FREDERICK WARNE & CO., INC.

NEW YORK AND LONDON

PRINTED IN THE U.S.A. BY A. HOEN & CO.

3 4 5 82 81 80 79 78

THE TALE OF
THE FAITHFUL DOVE

THERE is a town—a little old red-roofed town, a city of gates and walls. It has steep cobbled streets that go up, like the ribs of a crown; and a gray flint church on the summit.

The gold weather-cock glitters in the sunshine, and the pigeons wheel round it in quick short flights. As they turn and tumble, their wings gleam white against the thunder clouds over the sea.

On hot harvest days they fly out to the cornfields; but always with an eye on safety and their nests high up in the Ypres Tower —and the other eye for the falcons across the marsh at Camber.

But more often they are pecking about in the grass-grown streets, amongst the cobble stones of the market place or in the dusty yard of the windmill by the river.

"Why should a pigeon risk his tail in Winchelsea Marsh, while there is corn in Rye?" said Mr. Tidler, bobbing and bowing and strutting around.

"*My* ancestors were Antwerps. *We* carried messages for the smugglers. My great great grandfather used to cross the Channel twice a fortnight in a fishing boat, Mr. Tidler!" replied Amabella, preening her wings.

"My love, your great great grandmother was a tumbler!" said Mr. Tidler.

But although Mr. Tidler had differences with his wife Amabella, they were a most devoted pair, after the habit of pigeons who marry for life. They made their nest of rubbishy twigs and straws in a hole on the Ypres tower, where the wallflowers grow.

Amabella had laid an egg in the nest. She had left it and was sunning herself on a

broad flat stone at the edge of the battlements.

Mr. Tidler was hurrying up and down and round and round, cooing excitedly, turning in his bright pink toes, and bobbing and bowing, regardless of the complete inattention of his wife.

A score of other doves slanted across the face of the cliff below—Amabella slid off the stone and followed them, with a sudden clapping of wings in the hot silent air.

It was Sunday; but indeed even on week days the little old town seems always asleep. The sea has slipped away across the marsh and left it stranded, and it dozes through the lazy summer days like the Castle of Sleeping Beauty.

But the doves are not "asleep upon the house top." They are down in the Miller's yard, outside West Gate on the Winchelsea Road.

There are a dozen red and particoloured tumblers, black and white nuns, ruffled jacobins, and dusky blue-rocks, trampling about and bobbing their heads as they gobble up the grain.

Mrs. Tidler is in the thick of it, very hungry and pick peck pecketting.

Mr. Tidler is on the outskirts, anxious and indignant, but still bobbing and bowing.

"When a person has laid an egg, a person should *not* leave the fortifications," said Mr. Thomas Tidler.

He himself spent much of his time doing fancy steps on the long black muzzle of a rusty French gun.

"My great grand-uncle carried little screws

ot paper twisted round his leg between Rye and Sandwich," said Amabella.

"Why should we stay within walls in times of peace?" asked a little white dove.

Mr. Tidler had just tripped over a straw, and before he had time to gather himself together, to reply in argument—something came round the sails of the windmill like a thunder bolt.

Down went the little white dove; and then up and away in the claws of a peregrine falcon.

The falcon's mate was following close behind; he only missed his mark because he hesitated whether to strike Mr. or Mrs. Tidler.

He swept between them undecided and wheeled up in circles over the mill, ready for a fresh swoop at the pigeons as they raced back into the town.

The short winged doves threaded their way amongst the sheds with sudden twists and turns, flying low and dodging into the streets, where they hoped that the peregrine would not follow them.

One of them in its terror dashed in at an open window.

The cock pigeon with pathetic senseless courage flew behind his wife, to keep between her and the danger.

But alas, the tiercel* was a judge of pigeon-pie, and he had taken a fancy for the plumpness of Amabella! He singled out his intended victim, and ignored the other pigeons.

---

* Falconers call the female peregrine "the falcon"; she is much larger than the male bird, who is known as the "tiercel." There used to be peregrine falcons at Camber Castle; I don't think they breed there now; but there are still a few about the chalk cliffs on the south coast.

Twice he missed his stroke, as she dodged frantically amongst the chimney stacks; most unaccountably missed the second time, when Amabella's fate seemed sealed!

But Mrs. Tidler reverted to the habit of her ancestral relations—she gave an unmistakable "tumble" and mysteriously disappeared.

The peregrine, overshooting his mark, found himself above the church, where he was disconcerted by the sweet strains of the organ.

He soared upwards high over the town and away across the marsh.

Mr. Tidler, panting and scared almost to death—tumbled into a holly bush in the church yard.

The congregation was just coming out, "There do have been a hawk after them pigeons," remarked the sexton.

Mr. Tidler wished that the hawk had taken *him* instead of the little white dove, when he could not find Amabella. Pigeons are not very intelligent but they are unusually faithful.

He flew back to the Ypres Tower, in faint hope that she might have slipped home by Watch Bell Lane. But the nest was deserted and the egg was cold.

Mr. Tidler could not bear to look at it, he did not go near it again.

He wandered about the red tiled roofs, moping and disconsolate. At night he roosted on the ridge of the church, all out in the rain.

A white owl came and looked at him and seemed about to make a remark; but it changed its mind and went away.

Next day Mr. Tidler ate nothing and

moped; his draggled appearance attracted the attention of a black tom cat. It climbed on the roof of a shed in the street called "The Mint," with the intention of catching him.

Mr. Tidler flopped languidly across the road on to another roof, and mourned for Amabella.

Amabella's history was simple.

In twisting and ducking amongst the chimney stacks to escape from the peregrine, she had—half by accident—half on purpose—dived down the mouth of a tall red chimney pot.

The chimney belonged to the garret of an empty house, and the fireplace was stuffed up with a sack.

Mrs. Tidler, breathless and terrified, fell down upon the sack, and lay there comfortably enough.

There was sufficient room for her to stand up and flap her wings when she recovered. But it was impossible for her to fly upwards and out at the chimney-pot three yards above her head—a little circle of blue sky and scudding clouds over a shaft of darkness.

It is one thing to dive down a narrow hole with the wings closed; and quite another matter to mount—as a pigeon does—with beating wings and in circles.

Amabella was trapped!

She had a good deal of corn in her crop, which sustained her during the first night.

And next morning she laid another egg.

She made a satisfactory warm nest for it in the sack, and commenced to sit.

"I shall have to sit here for seventeen days," said Amabella with contented resignation.

But towards night she began to get hungry. And by the time that the stars came out and peeped down the chimney—Amabella was decidedly faint.

Once she woke up suddenly and saw a queer round face looking down upon her as she sat on her nest. Amabella thought that it was the moon; but it was a white owl.

And there were strange noises in the garret of the empty house, noises of a very very little squeaky fiddle, and noises of pattering and dancing, and the buzzing of blue bottle flies in the middle of the night.

Amabella between dreaming and fainting cooed drowsily to the music.

Early in the morning while she dozed upon her nest, there came a scrambling amongst the bricks of the chimney place—

"Who was that cooing to my dancers?

Who has been making music in my chimney?" asked a little old mouse.

"For the love of wheat and barley, send a message to Mr. Tidler! I cannot leave my egg, I cannot get out to feed! I am starving, Madam Mouse!" said Amabella.

The mouse, who was very small and old and dressed in antique fashion, in a silk gown with lace ruffles, examined Mrs. Tidler through a pair of tortoiseshell glasses.

"Indeed, Madam, I commiserate with you. I have had no experience in laying eggs; but I comprehend the pangs of hunger. The Ypres Tower? I will despatch a messenger at Cockcrow. I fear that I have no refreshment to offer to you Madam," added the friendly mouse. "This is an empty house, and we are church mice. We removed to our present abode on account of the owls.

I am a mouse of genteel descent," said she, smoothing her faded silk petticoat.

Amabella thanked her warmly. She was revived by friendship and described the exploits of her own ancestors the Antwerp carriers—

"You do not say so, Madam? The lace of these ruffles was smuggled; my great great grandmother found it in the secret recess of an old bureau—"

"You interest me extremely, Madam; *my* great great great great grandfather was cellar-mouse in the house of a Huguenot grocer."

"You may command my services; I will despatch a dozen starlings. They shall scour the roofs of Rye for Mr. Tidler."

So it happened that in the gray dawn of the second morning Mr. Tidler moping and dozing upon the roof of Rye Town Hall was aroused by a cock starling.

It pecked him, and directed him, half awake to the top of a tall red chimney pot in Mermaid Street.

"Bless my tail and toes! Amabella, my love? Amabella?" exclaimed Mr. Tidler, strutting round the top of the chimney-pot, and craning over the abyss, at imminent risk of falling in head foremost.

"Leave off that ridiculous noise, and fetch me corn at once! I have laid an egg," said Mrs. Tidler in smothered tones below.

So for more than two weeks day by day industriously, Mr. Tidler picked up corn for two—for two? enough for half a dozen; it would have filled a sack!

He collected such quantities in his ardour, and with such boldness, that folks talked about him in the market. They threw him

handfuls of grain, and wondered to see him fly away with it and return presently with an empty crop for more and more.

In and out between the horses' feet, under carts and barrows, or perching fearlessly on an open sack to sample the oats—bobbing and bowing his thanks—there seemed to be no limit to the appetite and industry of Mr. Tidler.

He flew backwards and forwards to the chimney pot and dropped in the grain.

All day long he either carried corn, or strutted round and round the top of the pot, cooing to the imprisoned Amabella.

At night he roosted on the pot with his tail inside, and cooed in his sleep.

The church mice grew quite fat in that empty house. And so did Mrs. Tidler, and so did her son who had hatched out of the egg.

"I have called him Tobias, Mr. Tidler," cooed Mrs. Tidler down below.

"You have called him nothing of the sort, Amabella. He shall be named Toby. Your great great grandmother was a tumbler!" replied Mr. Tidler strutting round and round up above, and shutting out half the sky.

"How shall we ever get out? He will be ready to fly tomorrow," said Mrs. Tidler.

"Do you see ere a blue-rock dove up thur? He do pick up corn by the bushel, and carries it up by yonder?" the sexton down in the road called up to a plumber and his boy, at work on a leaking roof.

"A cock blue-rock? He's been strutting and bobbing these two hours on a chimney-pot in Mermaid Street. Curtchying into the chimney, like as if he were looking for a sweep!" added the plumber with aroused curiosity.

"Hop across Tom, and take a look."

The apprentice scrambled over two intervening roofs, clattering over the tiles.

The starlings who nest in the gables flew out, scolding and screaming; and Mr. Tidler paused in his dance.

The sexton went round into Mermaid Street and watched from the opposite pavement, while the boy climbed upon the chimney stack of the empty house.

Mr. Tidler stuck to his post in speechless indignation; he threw himself into an attitude of defiance, with one wing raised in the air.

When the intruder stooped over the pot to look down—Mr. Tidler rose upon his toes with a hinnying noise, and slapped his wings across the boy's face, knocking off his cap which fell into the chimney.

"He's been and gone and done it!" chuckled the sexton. "Climb in at the garret window, lad; the catch is broken."

Tom scrambled cautiously down the roof. Mr. Tidler remained on the chimney pot, uttering angry crows, and puffing out his neck.

Amabella and her son down below were hissing and slapping at the cap, which had fallen on the top of them.

The catch of the old fashioned leaded window gave way with a push, and the boy stepped down into the garret through the cobwebs.

"Here be corn for sure; but it be shelled?" said Tom, looking round in perplexity at the piles of husks, relics of the supper parties of the friends of Madam Mouse.

He pulled the sack out of the fireplace. It

was followed by a stream of grain and mortar and dirt.

On the top of it came his cap, and Mrs. Tidler and her son, hissing and flapping and dazzled with the sudden return to daylight.

Tom drove the young pigeon into a corner and caught it.

Amabella bounced out at the window. The boy got out and climbed up the roof again, pursued by the two old pigeons, who flew wildly round his head.

"He be a right fat 'un!" said Tom, holding up his prize.

"I loikes pigeon poy!" said the objectionable plumber, leaning over the chimneys of the next door roof.

"He be a beauty to keep in a dove box," said Tom, stroking the even markings of the feathers—"*I* catched him?" he added sullenly.

Mr. Tidler in desperation dashed at him from behind, and knocked the cap over his eyes.

The boy clutched at the cap, and Toby slipped through his fingers, fluttering down the tiles till he lay in the spouting overhanging the street.

Mr. Tidler alighted on the water spout near him, he cooed and bobbed in wild defiance.

Amabella looked on from the house on the opposite side of the street; she was feeling stiff.

"I be afeared to follow him there, this roof be main rotten," said the boy.

"Butterfingers!" said the plumber.

Mr. Tidler taught his son to fly in the course of the afternoon. And Amabella ex-

ceedingly enjoyed a bath under the town
pump.

By the time she had preened and dried
her feathers, Toby was down in the road,
taking short flights and running after his
father, who was beside himself with ridiculous joy. He turned round and round in
circles, cooing with his head wrong side up,
and his bill on the ground.

They roosted at home in the Ypres Tower
that night.

And ever after Mr. Tidler bobbed and
bowed devotedly upon the battlements, in
proud admiration of his wife Amabella—